Good Luck, Martha

Adaptation by Karen Barss
Based on a TV series teleplay written by Raye Lankford
Based on the characters created by Susan Meddaugh

HOUGHTON MIFFLIN HARCOURT
Boston • New York • 2012

AGES	GRADES	GUIDED READING LEVEL	READING RECOVERY LEVEL	LEXILE® LEVEL
5–7	2	K	18	400L

For information about permission to reproduce selections from this book,
write to Permissions, Houghton Mifflin Harcourt Publishing Company,
215 Park Avenue South, New York, New York 10003.
Library of Congress Cataloging-in-Publication Data is on file.

ISBN: 978-0-547-57658-9 pb
ISBN: 978-0-547-57657-2 hc

Cover design by Rachel Newborn. Book design by Bill Smith Group.
www.hmhbooks.com
www.marthathetalkingdog.com

Manufactured in Singapore
TWP 10 9 8 7 6 5 4 3 2 1
4500323054

Helen and Carolina are going to the movies.
"It's called *The Curse of the Cursed*," Carolina tells Martha.
"Are you going to a movie with bad words in it?" Martha asks.

Helen laughs.
"Not that kind of curse," she says.
"When someone is cursed, it means they have bad luck."

Carolina stops and frowns.
"Like us," she says. "Look."
A ladder blocks their way.
"I won't walk under a ladder," she says.
"It's bad luck."

"That is just a superstition," says Helen.

"No, a superstition is a belief in something that is not real. Like magic."
"Oh, it is real," says Carolina. "It's really bad luck to walk under a ladder!"

Martha is not worried.
She walks back and forth under the ladder.
But then . . . oops! She bumps into it.

The bucket of paint spills!

"Maybe I do have bad luck," Martha says. "First the paint, now a bath."

Helen says, "You got splashed by paint. That was an accident."

"You mean I'm not cursed?" Martha says.
"Yippee!"
She dances around the bathroom.
But Martha knocks a mirror off a shelf.
It shatters!

Carolina gasps. "Seven years' bad luck!"
"Oh, woe," says Martha.

"What's wrong with Martha?" T.D. asks.
"She walked under a ladder and got
splashed with paint," says Helen.
"Then she broke a mirror. She thinks
she has bad luck."

T.D. sits next to Martha.

"Maybe the park will cheer you up," says T.D. They walk to the field to fly a kite.

"It could be worse," T.D. tells Martha. "I saw a movie about a guy who had such bad luck, it rubbed off on everybody else." Then T.D.'s kite gets stuck in a tree.

Martha says, "My bad luck is spreading too!"

As they walk home, they pass Mom outside her flower shop.

"Oh, dear," Mom says. "My flowers are wilted."

"It's my fault," Martha says, running away. "I'm cursed!"

Everywhere Martha goes that day, her bad luck follows . . . or so she thinks.

Martha walks up to Dad's bus and it gets a flat tire.

Martha says hello to Baby Jake and he falls.

Martha passes a roller skater.
He takes a tumble.

Martha passes a waiter with a tray of dishes.
She hears a crash!

That evening Helen is worried.
Martha has not come home for supper.
"Where are you going?" asks Mom.
"To find Martha," Helen says. "I think she
ran away."

Helen rides around town, looking
everywhere.

She is still looking when the sky
gets darker.

"I don't want my bad luck to rub off on you," Martha says.
"Superstitions are silly," Helen says.
"And curses are not real."

"What about the wilted flowers at the flower shop? And Dad's flat tire and Jake falling?" asks Martha.

Helen explains, "The sprinklers were not turned on. Dad's bus ran over a nail. And babies just fall down."
She pats Martha. "None of those things was your fault."

The sun comes out and Martha feels better. "Thanks, Helen," she says. "I guess it is silly to be superstitious. But I still believe in luck."

Because I'm sure lucky you're my friend!